Transformation

823 SHE

Transformation

Mary Shelley

ET REMOTISSIMA PROPE

Hesperus Classics

Hesperus Classics
Published by Hesperus Press Limited
4 Rickett Street, London SW6 1RU
www.hesperuspress.com

All three stories first published in *The Keepsake*: 'Transformation'
first published in 1831; 'The Mortal Immortal' first published in 1833;
'The Evil Eye' first published in 1829
First published by Hesperus Press Limited, 2004

Designed and typeset by Fraser Muggeridge
Printed in Italy by Graphic Studio Srl

ISBN: 1-84391-095-0

CONTENTS

Transformation

Forthwith this frame of mine was wrenched
With a woeful agony,
Which forced me to begin my tale,
And then it set me free.

Since then, at an uncertain hour,
That agony returns;
And till my ghastly tale is told
This heart within me burns.

Coleridge, *The Rime of the Ancient Mariner*

I have heard it said that when any strange, supernatural, and necromantic adventure has occurred to a human being, that being, however desirous he may be to conceal the same, feels at certain periods torn up as it were by an intellectual earthquake, and is forced to bare the inner depths of his spirit to another. I am a witness of the truth of this. I have dearly sworn to myself never to reveal to human ears the horrors to which I once, in excess of fiendly pride, delivered myself over. The holy man who heard my confession, and reconciled me to the church, is dead. None knows that once –

Why should it not be thus? Why tell a tale of impious tempting of providence, and soul-subduing humiliation? Why? Answer me, you who are wise in the secrets of human nature! I only know that so it is; and in spite of strong resolve – of a pride that too much masters me – of shame, and even of fear, so to render myself odious to my species – I must speak.

Genoa! My birthplace – proud city! Looking upon the blue waves of the Mediterranean Sea – do you remember me in my boyhood, when your cliffs and promontories, your bright sky and gay vineyards, were my world? Happy time! When to the young heart the narrow-bounded universe, which leaves, by its very limitation, free scope to the imagination, enchains our physical energies and, sole period in our lives, innocence and enjoyment are united. Yet, who can look back to childhood and not remember its sorrows and its harrowing fears? I was born with the most imperious, haughty, tameless spirit with which ever mortal was gifted. I quailed before my father only; and he, generous and noble, but capricious and tyrannical, at once fostered and checked the wild impetuosity of my character, making obedience necessary, but inspiring no respect for the motives which guided his commands. To be a man – free, independent or, in better words, insolent and domineering – was the hope and prayer of my rebel heart.

My father had one friend, a wealthy Genoese noble who, in a political tumult, was suddenly sentenced to banishment, and his property confiscated. The Marchese Torella went into exile alone. Like my father, he was a widower: he had one child, the almost infant Juliet, who was left under my father's guardianship. I should certainly have been an unkind master to the lovely girl, but that I was forced by my position to become her protector. A variety of childish incidents all tended to one point – to make Juliet see in me a rock of refuge; I, in her, one who must perish through the soft sensibility of her nature too rudely visited, but for my guardian care. We grew up together. The opening rose in May was not more sweet than this dear girl. An irradiation of beauty was spread prodigal feasts, now shedding blood in rivalry – were blind to the miserable state of their country and the dangers that impended over it, and gave themselves wholly up to dissolute enjoyment or savage strife. My character still followed me. I was arrogant and self-willed; I loved display, and above all, I threw all control far from me. Who could control me in Paris? My young friends were eager to foster passions which furnished them with pleasures. I was deemed handsome – I was master of every knightly accomplishment. I was disconnected with any political party. I grew a favourite with all; my presumption and arrogance were pardoned in one so young; I became a spoilt child. Who could control me? Not the letters and advice of Torella. Only strong necessity visiting me in the abhorred shape of an empty purse. But there were means to refill this void. Acre after acre, estate after estate, I sold. My dress, my jewels, my horses and their caparisons, were almost unrivalled in gorgeous Paris, while the lands of my inheritance passed into possession of others.

The Duke of Orleans was waylaid and murdered by the Duke of Burgundy. Fear and terror possessed all Paris. The Dauphin and the Queen shut themselves up; every pleasure was suspended. I grew weary of this state of things, and my heart yearned for my boyhood's haunts. I was nearly a beggar, yet still I would go there, claim my bride, and rebuild my fortunes. A few happy ventures as a merchant would make me rich again. Nevertheless, I would not return in humble guise. My last act was to dispose of my remaining estate near Albaro[2] for half its worth, for ready money. Then I despatched all kinds of artificers, arras, furniture of regal splendour, to fit up the last relic of my inheritance, my palace in Genoa. I lingered a little longer yet, ashamed at the part of the prodigal returned, which I feared I should play. I sent my horses. One matchless Spanish jennet I despatched to my promised bride; its caparisons flamed with jewels and cloth of gold. In every part I caused to be entwined the initials of Juliet and her Guido. My present found favour in her and in her father's eyes.

Still, to return a proclaimed spendthrift, the mark of impertinent wonder, perhaps of scorn, and to encounter singly the reproaches or taunts of my fellow-citizens, was no alluring prospect. As a shield between me and censure, I invited some few of the most reckless of my comrades to accompany me: thus I went armed against the world, hiding a rankling feeling, half fear and half penitence by bravado and an insolent display of satisfied vanity.

I arrived in Genoa. I trod the pavement of my ancestral palace. My proud step was no interpreter of my heart, for I deeply felt that, though surrounded by every luxury, I was a beggar. The first step I took in claiming Juliet must widely declare me such. I read contempt or pity in the looks of all. I fancied, so apt is conscience to imagine what it deserves, that rich and poor, young and old, all regarded me with derision. Torella came not near me. No wonder that my second father should expect a son's deference from me in waiting first on him. But, galled and stung by a sense of my follies and demerit, I strove to throw the blame on others. We kept nightly orgies in Palazzo Carega. To sleepless, riotous nights, followed listless, supine mornings. At the Ave Maria we showed our dainty persons in the streets, scoffing at the sober citizens, casting insolent glances on the shrinking women. Juliet was not among them – no, no; if she had been there, shame would have driven me away, if love had not brought me to her feet.

I grew tired of this. Suddenly I paid the Marchese a visit. He was at his villa, one among the many which deck the suburb of San Pietro d'Arena. It was the month of May – the blossoms of the fruit trees were fading among thick, green foliage; the vines were shooting forth; the ground strewn with the fallen olive blooms; the firefly was in the myrtle hedge; heaven and earth wore a mantle of surpassing beauty. Torella welcomed me kindly, though seriously; and even his shade of displeasure soon wore away. Some resemblance to my father – some look and tone of youthful ingenuousness, lurking still in spite of my misdeeds – softened the good old man's heart. He sent for his daughter – he presented me to her as her betrothed. The chamber became hallowed by a holy light as she entered. Hers was that cherub look – those large, soft eyes, full dimpled cheeks, and mouth of infantine sweetness that expresses the rare union of happiness and love. Admiration first possessed me. She is mine! was the second proud emotion, and my lips curled with haughty triumph. I had not been the *enfant gâté*[3] of the beauties of France not to have learnt the art of pleasing the soft heart of woman. If towards men I was overbearing, the deference I paid to them was the more in contrast. I commenced my courtship by the display of a thousand gallantries to Juliet who, vowed to me from infancy, had never admitted the devotion of others; and who, though accustomed to expressions of admiration, was uninitiated in the language of lovers.

8

For a few days all went well. Torella never alluded to my extravagance; he treated me as a favourite son. But the time came, as we discussed the preliminaries to my union with his daughter, when this fair face of things should be overcast. A contract had been drawn up in my father's lifetime. I had rendered this, in fact, void, by having squandered the whole of the wealth which was to have been shared by Juliet and myself. Torella, in consequence, chose to consider this bond as cancelled, and proposed another, in which, though the wealth he bestowed was immeasurably increased, there were so many restrictions as to the mode of spending it, that I, who saw independence only in free career being given to my own imperious will, taunted him as taking advantage of my situation, and refused utterly to subscribe to his conditions. The old man mildly strove to recall me to reason. Roused pride became the tyrant of my thought: I listened with indignation – I repelled him with disdain.

'Juliet, you are mine! Did we not interchange vows in our innocent childhood? Are we not one in the sight of God? And shall your cold-hearted, cold-blooded father divide us? Be generous, my love, be just; take not away a gift, last treasure of your Guido – retract not your vows – let us defy the world, and setting at nought the calculations of age, find in our mutual affection a refuge from every ill.'

Fiend I must have been, with such sophistry to endeavour to poison that sanctuary of holy thought and tender love. Juliet shrank from me affrighted. Her father was the best and kindest of men, and she strove to show me how, in obeying him, every good would follow. He would receive my tardy submission with warm affection; and generous pardon would follow my repentance. Profitless words for a young and gentle daughter to use to a man accustomed to make his will law, and to feel in his own heart a despot so terrible and stern that he could yield obedience to nought save his own imperious desires! My resentment grew with resistance; my wild companions were ready to add fuel to the flame. We laid a plan to carry off Juliet. At first it appeared to be crowned with success. Midway, on our return, we were overtaken by the agonised father and his attendants. A conflict ensued. Before the city guard came to decide the victory in favour of our antagonists, two of Torella's servitors were dangerously wounded.

This portion of my history weighs most heavily with me. Changed man as I am, I abhor myself in the recollection. May none who hear this tale ever have felt as I. A horse driven to fury by a rider armed with barbed spurs was not more a slave than I to the violent tyranny of my temper. A fiend possessed my soul, irritating it to madness. I felt the voice of conscience within me; but if I yielded to it for a brief interval, it was only to be a moment after torn, as by a whirlwind, away – borne along on the stream of desperate rage – the plaything of the storms engendered by pride. I was imprisoned, and at the instance of Torella, set free. Again I returned to carry off both him and his child to France; which hapless country, then preyed on by freebooters and gangs of lawless soldiery, offered a grateful refuge to a criminal like me. Our plots were discovered. I was sentenced to banishment; and as my debts were already enormous, my remaining property was put in the hands of commissioners for their was to be done? Should I crouch before my foe, and sue for forgiveness? Die rather ten thousand deaths! Never should they obtain that victory! Hate – I swore eternal hate! Hate from whom? To whom? From a wandering outcast to a mighty noble. I and my feelings were nothing to them: already had they forgotten one so unworthy. And Juliet! – her angel face and sylphlike form gleamed among the clouds of my despair with vain beauty; for I had lost her – the glory and flower of the world! Another will call her his! That smile of paradise will bless another!

Even now my heart fails within me when I recur to this rout of grim-visaged ideas. Now subdued almost to tears, now raving in my agony, still I wandered along the rocky shore, which grew at each step wilder and more desolate. Hanging rocks and hoar precipices overlooked the tideless ocean; black caverns yawned; and forever, among the seaworn recesses, murmured and dashed the unfruitful waters. Now my way was almost barred by an abrupt promontory, now rendered nearly impracticable by fragments fallen from the cliff. Evening was at hand, when, seaward, arose, as if on the waving of a wizard's wand, a murky web of clouds, blotting the late azure sky, and darkening and disturbing the till now placid deep. The clouds had strange fantastic shapes; and they changed, and mingled, and seemed to be driven about by a mighty spell. The waves raised their white crests; the thunder first muttered, then roared from across the waste of waters, which took a deep purple dye, flecked with foam. The spot where I stood, looked, on one side, to the widespread ocean; on the other, it was barred by a rugged promontory. Round this cape suddenly came, driven by the wind, a vessel. In vain the mariners tried to force a path for her to the open sea – the gale drove her on the rocks. It will perish! All on board will perish! Would I were among them! And to my young heart the idea of death came for the first time blended with that of joy. It was an awful sight to behold that vessel struggling with her fate. Hardly could I discern the sailors, but I heard them. It was soon all over! A rock, just covered by the tossing waves, and so unperceived, lay in wait for its prey. A crash of thunder broke over my head at the moment that, with a frightful shock, the skiff dashed upon her unseen enemy. In a brief space of time she went to pieces. There I stood in safety; and there were my fellow-creatures, battling, how hopelessly, with annihilation. I thought I saw them struggling – too truly did I hear their shrieks, conquering the barking surges in their shrill agony. The dark breakers threw hither and thither the fragments of the wreck: soon it disappeared. I had been fascinated to gaze till the end: at last I sank on my knees – I covered my face with my hands: I again looked up; something was floating on the billows towards the shore. It neared and neared. Was that a human form? – It grew more distinct; and at last a mighty wave, lifting the whole freight, lodged it upon a rock. A human being bestriding a sea chest! A human being! Yet was it one? Surely never such had existed before – a misshapen dwarf, with squinting eyes, distorted features, and body deformed, till it became a horror to behold. My blood, lately warming towards a fellow-being so snatched from a watery tomb, froze in my heart. The dwarf got off his chest; he tossed his straight, straggling hair from his odious visage:

'By St Beelzebub!' he exclaimed, 'I have been well bested.' He looked round and saw me. 'Oh, by the fiend! Here is another ally of the mighty one. To what saint did you offer prayers, friend – if not to mine? Yet I remember you not on board.'

I shrank from the monster and his blasphemy. Again he questioned me, and I muttered some inaudible reply. He continued:

'Your voice is drowned by this dissonant roar. What a noise the big ocean makes! Schoolboys bursting from their prison are not louder than these waves set free to play. They disturb me. I will no more of their ill-timed brawling. Silence, hoary one! Winds, avaunt! – to your homes! Clouds, fly to the antipodes, and leave our heaven clear!'

As he spoke, he stretched out his two long lank arms, that looked like spider's claws, and seemed to embrace with them the expanse before him. Was it a miracle? The clouds became broken and fled; the azure sky first peeped out, and then was spread a calm field of blue above us; the stormy gale was exchanged to the softly breathing west; the sea grew calm; the waves dwindled to ripplets.

'I like obedience even in these stupid elements,' said the dwarf. 'How much more in the tameless mind of man! It was a well got-up storm, you must allow – and all of my own making.'

It was tempting providence to interchange talk with this magician. But power, in all its shapes, is venerable to man. Awe, curiosity, a clinging fascination, drew me towards him.

'Come, don't be frightened, friend,' said the wretch:

'I am good humoured when pleased; and something does please me in your well-proportioned body and handsome face, though you look a little woebegone. You have suffered a land- – I, a sea-wreck. Perhaps I can allay the tempest of your fortunes as I did my own. Shall we be friends?' And he held out his hand; I could not touch it. 'Well, then, companions – that will do as well. And now, while I rest after the buffeting I underwent just now, tell me why, young and gallant as you seem, you wander thus alone and downcast on this wild seashore.'

The voice of the wretch was screeching and horrid, and his contortions as he spoke were frightful to behold. Yet he did gain a kind of influence over me, which I could not master, and I told him my tale. When it was ended, he laughed long and loud: the rocks echoed back the sound: hell seemed yelling around me.

'Oh, you cousin of Lucifer!' said he; 'so you too have fallen through your pride; and, though bright as the son of morning, you are ready to give up your good looks, your bride, and your well-being, rather than submit to the tyranny of good. I honour your choice, by my soul! So you have fled, and yield the day; and mean to starve on these rocks, and to let the birds peck out your dead eyes, while your enemy and your betrothed rejoice in your ruin. Your pride is strangely akin to humility, I think.'

As he spoke, a thousand fanged thoughts stung me to the heart.

'What would you that I should do?' I cried.

'I! Oh, nothing, but lie down and say your prayers before you die. But, were I you, I know the deed that should be done.'

I drew near him. His supernatural powers made him an oracle in my eyes; yet a strange unearthly thrill quivered through my frame as I said, 'Speak! Teach me – what act do you advise?'

'Revenge yourself, man! Humble your enemies! Set your foot on the old man's neck, and possess yourself of his daughter!'

'To the east and west I turn,' cried I, 'and see no means! Had I gold, much could I achieve; but, poor and single, I am powerless.'

The dwarf had been seated on his chest as he listened to my story. Now he got off; he touched a spring – it flew open! What a mine of wealth – of blazing jewels, beaming gold, and pale silver – was displayed therein! A mad desire to possess this treasure was born within me.

'Doubtless,' I said, 'one so powerful as you could do all things.'

'Nay,' said the monster, humbly, 'I am less omnipotent than I seem. Some things I possess which you may covet; but I would give them all for a small share, or even for a loan of what is yours.'

'My possessions are at your service,' I replied, bitterly – 'my poverty, my exile, my disgrace – I make a free gift of them all.'

'Good! I thank you. Add one other thing to your gift, and my treasure is yours.'

'As nothing is my sole inheritance, what besides nothing would you have?'

'Your comely face and well-made limbs.'

I shivered. Would this all-powerful monster murder me? I had no dagger. I forgot to pray – but I grew pale.

'I ask for a loan, not a gift,' said the frightful thing: 'lend me your body for three days – you shall have mine to cage your soul the while, and in payment, my chest. What say you to the bargain? – Three short days.'

We are told that it is dangerous to hold unlawful talk; and well do I prove the same. Tamely written down, it may seem incredible that I should lend any ear to this proposition; but, in spite of his unnatural ugliness, there was something fascinating in a being whose voice could govern earth, air, and sea. I felt a keen desire to comply, for with that chest I could command the world. My only hesitation resulted from a fear that he would not be true to his bargain. Then, I thought, I shall soon die here on these lonely sands, and the limbs he covets will be mine no more – it is worth the chance. And, besides, I knew that, by all the rules of art-magic, there were formulas and oaths which none of its practisers dared break. I hesitated to reply; and he went on, now displaying his wealth, now speaking of the petty price he demanded, till it seemed madness to refuse. Thus is it: place our bark in the current of the stream, and down, over fall and cataract it is hurried; give up our conduct to the wild torrent of passion, and we are away, we know not whither.

He swore many an oath, and I adjured him by many a sacred name, till I saw this wonder of power, this ruler of the elements, shiver like an autumn leaf before my words; and as if the spirit spoke unwillingly and per force within him, at last he, with broken voice, revealed the spell whereby he might be obliged, did he wish to play me false, to render up the unlawful spoil. Our warm lifeblood must mingle to make and to mar the charm.

Enough of this unholy theme. I was persuaded – the thing was done. The morrow dawned upon me as I lay upon the shingles, and I knew not my own shadow as it fell from me. I felt myself changed to a shape of horror, and cursed my easy faith and blind credulity. The chest was there – there the gold and precious stones for which I had sold the frame of flesh which nature had given me. The sight a little stilled my emotions: three days would soon be gone.

They did pass. The dwarf had supplied me with a plenteous store of food. At first I could hardly walk, so strange and out of joint were all my limbs; and my voice – it was that of the fiend. But I kept silent, and turned my face to the sun that I might not see my shadow, and counted the hours, and ruminated on my future conduct. To bring Torella to my feet – to possess my Juliet in spite of him – all this my wealth could easily achieve. During dark night I slept, and dreamt of the accomplishment of my desires. Two suns had set – the third dawned. I was agitated, fearful. Oh expectation, what a frightful thing are you, when kindled more by fear than hope! How do you twist yourself round the heart, torturing its pulsations! How do you dart unknown pangs all through our feeble mechanism, now seeming to shiver us like broken glass to nothingness, now giving us a fresh strength, which can do nothing, and so torments us by a sensation, such as the strong man must feel who cannot break his fetters though they bend in his grasp. Slowly paced the bright, bright orb up the eastern sky; long it lingered in the zenith, and still more slowly wandered down the west: it touched the horizon's verge – it was lost! Its glories were on the summits of the cliff – they grew dun and grey. The evening star shone bright. He will soon be here.

He came not! By the living heavens, he came not! – and night dragged out its weary length and, in its decaying age, 'day began to grizzle its dark hair'[4]; and the sun rose again on the most miserable wretch that ever upbraided its light. Three days thus I passed. The jewels and the gold – oh, how I abhorred them!

Well, well – I will not blacken these pages with de-moniac ravings. All too terrible were the thoughts, the raging tumult of ideas that filled my soul. At the end of that time I slept; I had not before since the third sunset; and I dreamt that I was at Juliet's feet, and she smiled, and then she shrieked – for she saw my transformation – and again she smiled, for still her beautiful lover knelt before her. But it was not I – it was he, the fiend, arrayed in my limbs, speaking with my voice, winning her with my looks of love. I strove to warn her, but my tongue refused its office; I strove to tear him from her, but I was rooted to the ground – I awoke with the agony. There were the solitary hoar precipices – there the plashing sea, the quiet strand, and the blue sky over all. What did it mean? Was my dream but a mirror of the truth? Was he wooing and winning my betrothed? I would on the instant back to Genoa – but I was banished. I laughed – the dwarf's yell burst from my lips – I, banished! Oh no! They had not exiled the foul limbs I wore; I might with these enter, without fear of incurring the threatened penalty of death, my own, my native city.

I began to walk towards Genoa. I was somewhat accustomed to my distorted limbs; none were ever so ill adapted for a straightforward movement; it was with infinite difficulty that I proceeded. Then, too, I desired to avoid all the hamlets strewn here and there on the sea beach, for I was unwilling to make a display of my hideousness. I was not quite sure that, if seen, the mere boys would not stone me to death, as I passed, for a monster; some ungentle salutations I did receive from the few peasants or fishermen I chanced to meet. But it was dark night before I approached Genoa. The weather was so balmy and sweet that it struck me that the Marchese and his daughter would very probably have quitted the city for their country retreat. It was from Villa Torella that I had attempted to carry off Juliet; I had spent many an hour reconnoitring the spot, and knew each inch of ground in its vicinity. It was beautifully situated, embosomed in trees, on the margin of a stream. As I drew near, it became evident that my conjecture was right; nay, moreover, that the hours were being then devoted to feasting and merriment. For the house was lit up; strains of soft and gay music were wafted towards me by the breeze. My heart sank within me. Such was the generous kindness of Torella's heart that I felt sure that he would not have indulged in public manifestations of rejoicing just after my unfortunate banishment, but for a cause I dared not dwell upon.

The country people were all alive and flocking about; it became necessary that I should study to conceal myself; and yet I longed to address someone, or to hear others discourse, or in any way to gain intelligence of what was really going on. At length, entering the walks that were in immediate vicinity to the mansion, I found one dark enough to veil my excessive frightfulness; and yet others as well as I were loitering in its shade. I soon gathered all I wanted to know – all that first made my very heart die with horror, and then boil with indignation. Tomorrow Juliet was to be given to the penitent, reformed, beloved Guido – tomorrow my bride was to pledge her vows to a fiend from hell! And I did this! My accursed pride – my demoniac violence and wicked self-idolatry had caused this act. For if I had acted as the wretch who had stolen my form had acted – if, with a mien at once yielding and dignified, I had presented myself to Torella, saying, 'I have done wrong, forgive me; I am unworthy of your angel-child, but permit me to claim her hereafter, when my altered conduct shall manifest that I abjure my vices, and endeavour to become in some sort worthy of her. I go to serve against the infidels; and when my zeal for religion and my true penitence for the past shall appear to you to cancel my crimes, permit me again to call myself your son.' Thus had he spoken; and the penitent was welcomed even as the prodigal son of scripture: the fatted calf was killed for him; and he, still pursuing the same path, displayed such open-hearted regret for his follies, so humble a concession of all his rights, and so ardent a resolve to reacquire them by a life of contrition and virtue, that he quickly conquered the kind, old man; and full pardon and the gift of his lovely child followed in swift succession.

Oh, had an angel from paradise whispered to me to act thus! But now, what would be the innocent Juliet's fate? Would God permit the foul union – or, some prodigy destroying it, link the dishonoured name of Carega with the worst of crimes? Tomorrow at dawn they were to be married: there was but one way to prevent this – to meet my enemy, and to enforce the ratification of our agreement. I felt that this could only be done by a mortal struggle. I had no sword – if indeed my distorted arms could wield a soldier's weapon – but I had a dagger, and in that lay my every hope. There was no time for pondering or balancing nicely the question: I might die in the attempt; but, besides the burning jealousy and despair of my own heart, honour, mere humanity, demanded that I should fall rather than not destroy the machinations of the fiend.

The guests departed – the lights began to disappear; it was evident that the inhabitants of the villa were seeking repose. I hid myself among the trees – the garden grew desert – the gates were closed – I wandered round and came under a window. Ah! Well did I know the same! – a soft twilight glimmered in the room – the curtains were half withdrawn. It was the temple of innocence and beauty. Its magnificence was tempered, as it were, by the slight disarrangements occasioned by its being dwelt in, and all the objects scattered around displayed the taste of her who hallowed it by her presence. I saw her enter with a quick light step – I saw her approach the window – she drew back the curtain yet further, and looked out into the night. Its breezy freshness played among her ringlets, and wafted them from the transparent marble of her brow. She clasped her hands, she raised her eyes to heaven. I heard her voice. 'Guido!' she softly murmured, 'Mine own Guido!' and then, as if overcome by the fullness of her own heart, she sank on her knees. Her upraised eyes – her negligent but graceful attitude – the beaming thankfulness that lit up her face – oh, these are tame words! Heart of mine, you imagest ever, though you cannot portray, the celestial beauty of that child of light and love.

I heard a step – a quick firm step along the shady avenue. Soon I saw a cavalier – richly dressed, young and, I thought, graceful to look on – advance. I hid myself yet closer. The youth approached; he paused beneath the window. She arose, and again looking out she saw him, and said – I cannot, no, at this distant time I cannot record her terms of soft silver tenderness; to me they were spoken, but they were replied to by him.

'I will not go,' he cried: 'here where you have been, where your memory glides like some heaven-visiting ghost, I will pass the long hours till we meet, never, my Juliet, again, day or night, to part. But do you, my love, retire; the cold morn and fitful breeze will make your cheek pale, and fill with languor your love-lit eyes. Ah, sweetest! Could I press one kiss upon them, I could, I think, repose.'

And then he approached still nearer, and I thought he was about to clamber into her chamber. I had hesitated, not to terrify her; now I was no longer master of myself. I rushed forward – I threw myself on him – I tore him away – I cried, 'O loathsome and foul-shaped wretch!'

I need not repeat epithets, all tending, as it appeared, to rail at a person I at present feel some partiality for. A shriek rose from Juliet's lips. I neither heard nor saw – I felt only mine enemy, whose throat I grasped, and my dagger's hilt; he struggled, but could not escape: at length hoarsely he breathed these words: 'Do! – strike home! Destroy this body – you will still live: may your life be long and merry!'

The descending dagger was arrested at the word, and

he, feeling my hold relax, extricated himself and drew his sword, while the uproar in the house, and flying of torches from one room to the other, showed that soon we should be separated. In the midst of my frenzy there was much calculation: fall I might, and so that he did not survive, I cared not for the death blow I might deal against myself. While still, therefore, he thought I paused, and while I saw the villainous resolve to take advantage of my hesitation, in the sudden thrust he made at me, I threw myself on his sword, and at the same moment plunged my dagger, with a true desperate aim, in his side. We fell together, rolling over each other, and the tide of blood that flowed from the gaping wound of each mingled on the grass. More I know not – I fainted.

Again I returned to life: weak almost to death, I found myself stretched upon a bed – Juliet was kneeling beside it. Strange! My first broken request was for a mirror. I was so wan and ghastly that my poor girl hesitated, as she told me afterwards; but, by the mass! I thought myself a right proper youth when I saw the dear reflection of my own well-known features. I confess it is a weakness, but I avow it, I do entertain a considerable affection for the countenance and limbs I behold whenever I look at a glass; and have more mirrors in my house, and consult them oftener than any beauty in Venice. Before you too much condemn me, permit me to say that no one better knows than I the value of his own body; no one, probably, except myself, ever having had it stolen from him.

Incoherently I at first talked of the dwarf and his crimes, and reproached Juliet for her too easy admission of his love. She thought me raving, as well she might, and yet it was some time before I could prevail on myself to admit that the Guido whose penitence had won her back for me was myself; and while I cursed bitterly the monstrous dwarf, and blessed the well-directed blow that had deprived him of life, I suddenly checked myself when I heard her say 'Amen!' knowing that him whom she reviled was my very self. A little reflection taught me silence – a little practice enabled me to speak of that frightful night without any very excessive blunder. The wound I had given myself was no mockery of one – it was long before I recovered – and as the benevolent and generous Torella sat beside me, talking such wisdom as might win friends to repentance, and mine own dear Juliet hovered near me, administering to my wants, and cheering me by her smiles, the work of my bodily cure and mental reform went on together. I have never, indeed, wholly recovered my strength – my cheek is paler since – my person a little bent. Juliet sometimes ventures to allude bitterly to the malice that caused this change, but I kiss her on the moment, and tell her all is for the best. I am a fonder and more faithful husband – and true is this – but for that wound, never had I called her mine.

I did not revisit the seashore, nor seek for the fiend's treasure; yet, while I ponder on the past, I often think, and my confessor was not backward in favouring the idea, that it might be a good rather than an evil spirit, sent by my guardian angel, to show me the folly and misery of pride. So well at least did I learn this lesson, roughly taught as I was, that I am known now by all my friends and fellow-citizens by the name of Guido il Cortese.[5]

NOTES

1. Charles VI (1368–1422), King of France, known as Charles the Foolish, reigned from 1380. He was defeated by Henry V at the Battle of Agincourt (1415).
2. Lido di Albaro is an area of Italy near Genoa's harbour.
3. Literally 'spoilt child', but here 'pampered darling'. (French)
4. From Lord Byron's *Werner* (1823), III.iv. 152–53.
5. Guido the Kind-Hearted. (Italian)

The Mortal Immortal

16th July 1833. This is a memorable anniversary for me; on it I complete my three hundred and twenty-third year!

The Wandering Jew?[1] Certainly not. More than eighteen centuries have passed over his head. In comparison with him, I am a very young immortal.

Am I, then, immortal? This is a question which I have asked myself, by day and night, for now three hundred and three years, and yet cannot answer it. I detected a grey hair amidst my brown locks this very day – that surely signifies decay. Yet it may have remained concealed there for three hundred years – for some persons have become entirely white-headed before twenty years of age.

I will tell my story, and my reader shall judge for me. I will tell my story, and so contrive to pass some few hours of a long eternity become so wearisome to me. For ever! Can it be? To live for ever! I have heard of enchantments in which the victims were plunged into a deep sleep, to wake, after a hundred years, as fresh as ever. I have heard of the Seven Sleepers – thus to be immortal would not be so burdensome. But oh! the weight of never-ending time – the tedious passage of the still-succeeding hours! How happy was the fabled Nourjahad![2] But to my task.

All the world has heard of Cornelius Agrippa.[3] His memory is as immortal as his arts have made me. All the world has also heard of his scholar, who, unawares, raised the foul fiend during his master's absence, and was destroyed by him.[4] The report, true or false, of this accident, was attended with many inconveniences to the renowned philosopher. All his scholars at once deserted him – his servants disappeared. He had no one near him to put coals on his ever-burning fires while he slept, or to attend to the changeful colours of his medicines while he studied. Experiment after experiment failed, because one pair of hands was insufficient to complete them: the dark spirits laughed at him for not being able to retain a single mortal in his service.

I was then very young – very poor – and very much in love. I had been for about a year the pupil of Cornelius, though I was absent when this accident took place. On my return, my friends implored me not to return to the alchemist's abode. I trembled as I listened to the dire tale they told; I required no second warning; and when Cornelius came and offered me a purse of gold if I would remain under his roof, I felt as if Satan himself tempted me. My teeth chattered – my hair stood on end. I ran off as fast as my trembling knees would permit.

My failing steps were directed whither for two years they had every evening been attracted – a gently bubbling spring of pure living waters, beside which lingered a dark-haired girl, whose beaming eyes were fixed on the path I was accustomed each night to tread. I cannot remember the hour when I did not love Bertha; we had been neighbours and playmates from infancy – her parents, like mine, were of humble life, yet respectable – our attachment had been a source of pleasure to them. In an evil hour, a malignant fever carried off both her father and mother, and Bertha became an orphan. She would have found a home beneath my paternal roof, but, unfortunately, the old lady of the near castle, rich, childless, and solitary, declared her intention to adopt her. Henceforth Bertha was clad in silk – inhabited a marble palace – and was looked on as being highly favoured by fortune. But in her new situation among her new associates, Bertha remained true to the friend of her humbler days; she often visited the cottage of my father, and when forbidden to go thither, she would stray towards the neighbouring wood, and meet me beside its shady fountain.

She often declared that she owed no duty to her new protectress equal in sanctity to that which bound us. Yet still I was too poor to marry, and she grew weary of being tormented on my account. She had a haughty but an impatient spirit, and grew angry at the obstacles that prevented our union. We met now after an absence, and she had been sorely beset while I was away; she complained bitterly, and almost reproached me for being poor. I replied hastily: 'I am honest, if I am poor! – were I not, I might soon become rich!'

This exclamation produced a thousand questions. I feared to shock her by owning the truth, but she drew it from me; and then, casting a look of disdain on me, she said: 'You pretend to love, and you fear to face the devil for my sake!'

I protested that I had only dreaded to offend her; while she dwelt on the magnitude of the reward that I should receive. Thus encouraged – shamed by her – led on by love and hope, laughing at my late fears, with quick steps and a light heart, I returned to accept the offers of the alchemist, and was instantly installed in my office.

A year passed away. I became possessed of no insignificant sum of money. Custom had banished my fears. In spite of the most painful vigilance, I had never detected the trace of a cloven foot; nor was the studious silence of our abode ever disturbed by demoniac howls. I still continued my stolen interviews with Bertha, and hope dawned on me – hope – but not perfect joy; for Bertha fancied that love and security were enemies, and her pleasure was to divide them in my bosom. Though true of heart, she was somewhat of a coquette in manner; and I was jealous as a Turk. She slighted me in a thousand ways, yet would never acknowledge herself to be in the wrong. She would drive me mad with anger, and then force me to beg her pardon. Sometimes she fancied that I was not sufficiently submissive, and then she had some story of a rival, favoured by her protectress. She was surrounded by silk-clad youths – the rich and gay. What chance had the sad-robed scholar of Cornelius compared with these?

On one occasion, the philosopher made such large demands upon my time that I was unable to meet her as I was wont. He was engaged in some mighty work, and I was forced to remain, day and night, feeding his furnaces and watching his chemical preparations. Bertha waited for me in vain at the fountain. Her haughty spirit fired at this neglect; and when at last I stole out during the few short minutes allotted to me for slumber, and hoped to be consoled by her, she received me with disdain, dismissed me in scorn, and vowed that any man should possess her hand rather than he who could not be in two places at once for her sake. She would be revenged! And truly she was. In my dingy retreat I heard that she had been hunting, attended by Albert Hoffer. Albert Hoffer was favoured by her protectress, and the three passed in cavalcade before my smoky window. I thought that they mentioned my name – it was followed by a laugh of derision, as her dark eyes glanced contemptuously towards my abode.

Jealousy, with all its venom, and all its misery, entered my breast. Now I shed a torrent of tears to think that I should never call her mine; and, anon, I imprecated a thousand curses on her inconstancy. Yet, still I must stir the fires of the alchemist, still attend on the changes of his unintelligible medicines.

Cornelius had watched for three days and nights, nor closed his eyes. The progress of his alembics was slower than he expected: in spite of his anxiety, sleep weighed upon his eyelids. Again and again he threw off drowsiness with more than human energy; again and again it stole away his senses. He eyed his crucibles wistfully. 'Not ready yet,' he murmured; 'will another night pass before the work is accomplished? Winzy, you are vigilant – you are faithful – you have slept, my boy – you slept last night. Look at that glass vessel. The liquid it contains is of a soft rose colour: the moment it begins to change its hue, awaken me – till then I may close my eyes. First, it will turn white, and then emit golden flashes; but wait not till then; when the rose colour fades, rouse me.' I scarcely heard the last words, muttered, as they were, in sleep. Even then he did not quite yield to nature. 'Winzy, my boy,' he again said, 'do not touch the vessel – do not put it to your lips; it is a philtre – a philtre to cure love; you would not cease to love your Bertha – beware to drink!'

And he slept. His venerable head sunk on his breast, and I scarce heard his regular breathing. For a few minutes I watched the vessel – the rosy hue of the liquid remained unchanged. Then my thoughts wandered – they visited the fountain, and dwelt on a thousand charming scenes never to be renewed – never! Serpents and adders were in my heart as the word 'Never!' half formed itself on my lips. False girl! – false and cruel! Never more would she smile on me as that evening she smiled on Albert. Worthless, detested woman! I would not remain unrevenged – she should see Albert expire at her feet – she should die beneath my vengeance. She had smiled in disdain and triumph – she knew my wretchedness and her power. Yet what power had she? The power of exciting my hate – my utter scorn – my – oh, all but indifference! Could I attain that – could I regard her with careless eyes, transferring my rejected love to one fairer and more true? That were indeed a victory!

A bright flash darted before my eyes. I had forgotten the medicine of the adept; I gazed on it with wonder: flashes of admirable beauty, more bright than those which the diamond emits when the sun's rays are on it, glanced from the surface of the liquid; an odour the most fragrant and grateful stole over my sense; the vessel seemed one globe of living radiance, lovely to the eye, and most inviting to the taste. The first thought, instinctively inspired by the grosser sense, was, 'I will – I must – drink.' I raised the vessel to my lips. 'It will cure me of love – of torture!' Already I had quaffed half of the most delicious liquor ever tasted by the palate of man, when the philosopher stirred. I started – I dropped the glass – the fluid flamed and glanced along the floor, while I felt Cornelius' gripe at my throat as he shrieked aloud, 'Wretch! you have destroyed the labour of my life!'

The philosopher was totally unaware that I had drunk

any portion of his drug. His idea was, and I gave a tacit assent to it, that I had raised the vessel from curiosity, and that, frightened at its brightness and the flashes of intense light it gave forth, I had let it fall. I never undeceived him. The fire of the medicine was quenched – the fragrance died away – he grew calm, as a philosopher should under the heaviest trials, and dismissed me to rest.

I will not attempt to describe the sleep of glory and bliss which bathed my soul in paradise during the remaining hours of that memorable night. Words would be faint and shallow types of my enjoyment, or of the gladness that possessed my bosom when I woke. I trod air – my thoughts were in heaven. Earth appeared heaven, and my inheritance upon it was to be one trance of delight. 'This it is to be cured of love,' I thought; 'I will see Bertha this day, and she will find her lover cold and regardless: too happy to be disdainful, yet how utterly indifferent to her!'

The hours danced away. The philosopher, secure that he had once succeeded, and believing that he might again, began to concoct the same medicine once more. He was shut up with his books and drugs, and I had a holiday. I dressed myself with care; I looked in an old but polished shield which served me for a mirror; I thought my good looks had wonderfully improved. I hurried beyond the precincts of the town; joy in my soul, the beauty of heaven and earth around me. I turned my steps towards the castle – I could look on its lofty turrets with lightness of heart, for I was cured of love. My Bertha saw me afar off as I came up the avenue. I know not what sudden impulse animated her bosom, but at the sight, she sprung with a light fawn-like bound down the marble steps, and was hastening towards me. But I had been perceived by another person. The old high-born hag, who called herself her protectress, and was her tyrant, had seen me, also; she hobbled, panting, up the terrace; a page, as ugly as herself, held up her train, and fanned her as she hurried along, and stopped my fair girl with a 'How, now, my bold mistress? Whither so fast? Back to your cage – hawks are abroad!'

Bertha clasped her hands – her eyes were still bent on my approaching figure. I saw the contest. How I abhorred the old crone who checked the kind impulses of my Bertha's softening heart. Hitherto, respect for her rank had caused me to avoid the lady of the castle; now I disdained such trivial considerations. I was cured of love, and lifted above all human fears; I hastened forwards, and soon reached the terrace. How lovely Bertha looked! Her eyes flashing fire, her cheeks glowing with impatience and anger, she was a thousand times more graceful and charming than ever – I no longer loved – Oh! no, I adored – worshipped – idolised her!

She had that morning been persecuted, with more than usual vehemence, to consent to an immediate marriage with my rival. She was reproached with the encouragement that she had shown him – she was threatened with being turned out of doors with disgrace and shame. Her proud spirit rose in arms at the threat; but when she remembered the scorn that she had heaped upon me, and how, perhaps, she had thus lost one whom she now regarded as her only friend, she wept with remorse and rage. At that moment I appeared. 'O, Winzy!' she exclaimed, 'take me to your mother's cot; swiftly let me leave the detested luxuries and wretchedness of this noble dwelling – take me to poverty and happiness.'

I clasped her in my arms with transport. The old lady was speechless with fury, and broke forth into invective only when we were far on our road to my natal cottage. My mother received the fair fugitive, escaped from a gilt cage to nature and liberty, with tenderness and joy; my father, who loved her, welcomed her heartily; it was a day of rejoicing, which did not need the addition of the celestial potion of the alchemist to steep me in delight.

Soon after this eventful day, I became the husband of Bertha. I ceased to be the scholar of Cornelius, but I continued his friend. I always felt grateful to him for having, unawares, procured me that delicious draught of a divine elixir, which, instead of curing me of love (sad cure! solitary and joyless remedy for evils which seem blessings to the memory), had inspired me with courage and resolution, thus winning for me an inestimable treasure in my Bertha.

I often called to mind that period of trancelike inebriation with wonder. The drink of Cornelius had not fulfilled the task for which he affirmed that it had been prepared, but its effects were more potent and blissful than words can express.

They had faded by degrees, yet they lingered long – and painted life in hues of splendour. Bertha often wondered at my lightness of heart and unaccustomed gaiety; for, before, I had been rather serious, or even sad, in my disposition. She loved me the better for my cheerful temper, and our days were winged by joy.

Five years afterwards I was suddenly summoned to

the bedside of the dying Cornelius. He had sent for me in haste, conjuring my instant presence. I found him stretched on his pallet, enfeebled even to death; all of life that yet remained animated his piercing eyes, and they were fixed on a glass vessel, full of a roseate liquid.

'Behold,' he said, in a broken and inward voice, 'the vanity of human wishes! A second time my hopes are about to be crowned, a second time they are destroyed. Look at that liquor – you remember five years ago I had prepared the same, with the same success; then, as now, my thirsting lips expected to taste the immortal elixir – you dashed it from me! And at present it is too late.'

He spoke with difficulty, and fell back on his pillow. I could not help saying:

'How, revered master, can a cure for love restore you to life?'

A faint smile gleamed across his face as I listened earnestly to his scarcely intelligible answer. 'A cure for love and for all things – the Elixir of Immortality. Ah! If now I might drink, I should live for ever!'

As he spoke, a golden flash gleamed from the fluid; a well-remembered fragrance stole over the air; he raised himself, all weak as he was – strength seemed miraculously to re-enter his frame – he stretched forth his hand – a loud explosion startled me – a ray of fire shot up from the elixir, and the glass vessel which contained it was shivered to atoms! I turned my eyes towards the philosopher; he had fallen back – his eyes were glassy – his features rigid – he was dead!

But I lived, and was to live for ever! So said the unfortunate alchemist, and for a few days I believed his words. I remembered the glorious drunkenness that had followed my stolen draught. I reflected on the change I had felt in my frame – in my soul. The bounding elasticity of the one – the buoyant lightness of the other. I surveyed myself in a mirror, and could perceive no change in my features during the space of the five years which had elapsed. I remembered the radiant hues and grateful scent of that delicious beverage – worthy the gift it was capable of bestowing – I was, then, IMMORTAL!

A few days after, I laughed at my credulity. The old proverb, that 'a prophet is least regarded in his own country,'[5] was true with respect to me and my defunct master. I loved him as a man – I respected him as a sage – but I derided the notion that he could command the powers of darkness, and laughed at the superstitious fears with which he was regarded by the vulgar. He was a wise philosopher, but had no acquaintance with any spirits but those clad in flesh and blood. His science was simply human; and human science, I soon persuaded myself, could never conquer nature's laws so far as to imprison the soul for ever within its carnal habitation. Cornelius had brewed a soul-refreshing drink – more inebriating than wine – sweeter and more fragrant than any fruit: it possessed probably strong medicinal powers, imparting gladness to the heart and vigour to the limbs; but its effects would wear out; already were they diminished in my frame. I was a lucky fellow to have quaffed health and joyous spirits, and perhaps long life, at my master's hands; but my good fortune ended there: longevity was far different from immortality.

I continued to entertain this belief for many years. Sometimes a thought stole across me – was the alchemist indeed deceived? But my habitual credence was that I should meet the fate of all the children of Adam at my appointed time – a little late, but still at a natural age. Yet it was certain that I retained a wonderfully youthful look. I was laughed at for my vanity in consulting the mirror so often, but I consulted it in vain – my brow was untrenched – my cheeks – my eyes – my whole person continued as untarnished as in my twentieth year.

I was troubled. I looked at the faded beauty of Bertha – I seemed more like her son. By degrees our neighbours began to make similar observations, and I found at last that I went by the name of the 'scholar bewitched'. Bertha herself grew uneasy. She became jealous and peevish, and at length she began to question me. We had no children; we were all in all to each other; and though, as she grew older, her vivacious spirit became a little allied to ill-temper, and her beauty sadly diminished, I cherished her in my heart as the mistress I had idolised, the wife I had sought and won with such perfect love.

At last our situation became intolerable: Bertha was fifty – I twenty years of age. I had, in very shame, in some measure adopted the habits of a more advanced age; I no longer mingled in the dance among the young and gay, but my heart bounded along with them while I restrained my feet; and a sorry figure I cut among the Nestors[6] of our village. But before the time I mention, things were altered – we were universally shunned; we were – at least, I was – reported to have kept up an iniquitous acquaintance with some of my former master's supposed friends. Poor

Bertha was pitied, but deserted. I was regarded with horror and detestation.

What was to be done? We sat by our winter fire – poverty had made itself felt, for none would buy the produce of my farm; and often I had been forced to journey twenty miles, to some place where I was not known, to dispose of our property. It is true we had saved something for an evil day – that day was come.

We sat by our lone fireside – the old-hearted youth and his antiquated wife. Again Bertha insisted on knowing the truth; she recapitulated all she had ever heard said about me, and added her own observations. She conjured me to cast off the spell; she described how much more comely grey hairs were than my chestnut locks; she descanted on the reverence and respect due to age – how preferable to the slight regard paid to mere children: could I imagine that the despicable gifts of youth and good looks out-weighed disgrace, hatred, and scorn? Nay, in the end I should be burnt as a dealer in the black art, while she, to whom I had not deigned to communicate any portion of my good fortune, might be stoned as my accomplice. At length she insinuated that I must share my secret with her, and bestow on her like benefits to those I myself enjoyed, or she would denounce me – and then she burst into tears.

Thus beset, I thought it was the best way to tell the truth. I revealed it as tenderly as I could, and spoke only of a very long life, not of immortality – which representation, indeed, coincided best with my own ideas. When I ended, I rose and said:

'And now, my Bertha, will you denounce the lover of your youth? You will not, I know. But it is too hard, my poor wife, that you should suffer from my ill-luck and the accursed arts of Cornelius. I will leave you – you have wealth enough, and friends will return in my absence. I will go; young as I seem, and strong as I am, I can work and gain my bread among strangers, unsuspected and unknown. I loved you in youth; God is my witness that I would not desert you in age, but that your safety and happiness require it.'

I took my cap and moved towards the door; in a moment Bertha's arms were round my neck, and her lips were pressed to mine. 'No, my husband, my Winzy,' she said, 'you shall not go alone – take me with you; we will remove from this place, and, as you say, among strangers we shall be unsuspected and safe. I am not so very old as quite to shame you, my Winzy; and I dare say the charm will soon wear off, and, with the blessing of God, you will become more elderly looking, as is fitting; you shall not leave me.'

I returned the good soul's embrace heartily. 'I will not, my Bertha; but for your sake I had not thought of such a thing. I will be your true, faithful husband while you are spared to me, and do my duty by you to the last.'

The next day we prepared secretly for our emigration. We were obliged to make great pecuniary sacrifices – it could not be helped. We realised a sum sufficient, at least, to maintain us while Bertha lived; and, without saying adieu to anyone, quitted our native country to take refuge in a remote part of western France.

It was a cruel thing to transport poor Bertha from her native village and the friends of her youth to a new country, new language, new customs. The strange secret of

44

my destiny rendered this removal immaterial to me; but I compassionated her deeply, and was glad to perceive that she found compensation for her misfortunes in a variety of little ridiculous circumstances. Away from all telltale chroniclers, she sought to decrease the apparent disparity of our ages by a thousand feminine arts – rouge, youthful dress, and assumed juvenility of manner. I could not be angry. Did not I myself wear a mask? Why quarrel with hers, because it was less successful? I grieved deeply when I remembered that this was my Bertha, whom I had loved so fondly, and won with such transport – the dark-eyed, dark-haired girl, with smiles of enchanting archness and a step like a fawn – this mincing, simpering, jealous old woman. I should have revered her grey locks and withered cheeks; but thus! It was my work, I knew; but I did not the less deplore this type of human weakness.

Her jealousy never slept. Her chief occupation was to discover that, in spite of outward appearances, I was myself growing old. I verily believe that the poor soul loved me truly in her heart, but never had woman so tormenting a mode of displaying fondness. She would discern wrinkles in my face and decrepitude in my walk, while I bounded along in youthful vigour, the youngest looking of twenty youths. I never dared address another woman: on one occasion, fancying that the belle of the village regarded me with favouring eyes, she bought me a grey wig. Her constant discourse among her acquaintances was that though I looked so young, there was ruin at work within my frame; and she affirmed that the worst symptom about me was my apparent health. My youth was a disease, she said, and I ought at all times to prepare, if not for a sudden and awful death, at least to awake some morning white-headed and bowed down with all the marks of advanced years. I let her talk – I often joined in her conjectures. Her warnings chimed in with my never-ceasing speculations concerning my state, and I took an earnest, though painful, interest in listening to all that her quick wit and excited imagination could say on the subject.

Why dwell on these minute circumstances? We lived on for many long years. Bertha became bedridden and paralytic: I nursed her as a mother might a child. She grew peevish, and still harped upon one string – of how long I should survive her. It has ever been a source of consolation to me that I performed my duty scrupulously towards her. She had been mine in youth, she was mine in age, and at last, when I heaped the sod over her corpse, I wept to feel that I had lost all that really bound me to humanity.

Since then how many have been my cares and woes, how few and empty my enjoyments! I pause here in my history – I will pursue it no further. A sailor without rudder or compass, tossed on a stormy sea – a traveller lost on a widespread heath, without landmark or stone to guide him – such have I been: more lost, more hopeless than either. A nearing ship, a gleam from some far cot, may save them; but I have no beacon except the hope of death.

Death! Mysterious, ill-visaged friend of weak humanity! Why alone of all mortals have you cast me from your sheltering fold? Oh, for the peace of the grave! The deep silence of the iron-bound tomb! That thought would cease to work in my brain, and my heart beat no more with emotions varied only by new forms of sadness!

Am I immortal? I return to my first question. In the first place, is it not more probable that the beverage of the alchemist was fraught rather with longevity than eternal life? Such is my hope. And then be it remembered that I only drank half of the potion prepared by him. Was not the whole necessary to complete the charm? To have drained half the Elixir of Immortality is but to be half immortal – my 'for ever' is thus truncated and null.

But again, who shall number the years of the half of eternity? I often try to imagine by what rule the infinite may be divided. Sometimes I fancy age advancing upon me. One grey hair I have found. Fool! Do I lament? Yes, the fear of age and death often creeps coldly into my heart; and the more I live, the more I dread death, even while I abhor life. Such an enigma is man – born to perish – when he wars, as I do, against the established laws of his nature.

But for this anomaly of feeling surely I might die: the medicine of the alchemist would not be proof against fire – sword – and the strangling waters. I have gazed upon the blue depths of many a placid lake, and the tumultuous rushing of many a mighty river, and have said peace inhabits those waters; yet I have turned my steps away, to live yet another day. I have asked myself whether suicide would be a crime in one to whom thus only the portals of the other world could be opened. I have done all, except presenting myself as a soldier or duellist, an object of destruction to my – no, not my fellow-mortals, and therefore I have shrunk away. They are not my fellows. The inextinguishable power of life in my frame, and their ephemeral existence, place us wide as the poles asunder.

I could not raise a hand against the meanest or the most powerful among them.

Thus I have lived on for many a year – alone, and weary of myself – desirous of death, yet never dying – a mortal immortal. Neither ambition nor avarice can enter my mind, and the ardent love that gnaws at my heart, never to be returned – never to find an equal on which to expend itself – lives there only to torment me.

This very day I conceived a design by which I may end all – without self-slaughter, without making another man a Cain – an expedition, which mortal frame can never survive, even endued with the youth and strength that inhabits mine. Thus I shall put my immortality to the test, and rest for ever – or return, the wonder and benefactor of the human species.

Before I go, a miserable vanity has caused me to pen these pages. I would not die, and leave no name behind. Three centuries have passed since I quaffed the fatal beverage: another year shall not elapse before, encountering gigantic dangers – warring with the powers of frost in their home – beset by famine, toil, and tempest – I yield this body, too tenacious a cage for a soul which thirsts for freedom, to the destructive elements of air and water – or, if I survive, my name shall be recorded as one of the most famous among the sons of men; and, my task achieved, I shall adopt more resolute means, and, by scattering and annihilating the atoms that compose my frame, set at liberty the life imprisoned within, and so cruelly prevented from soaring from this dim earth to a sphere more congenial to its immortal essence.

NOTES

1. References to the Wandering Jew are common in literature. Samuel Taylor Coleridge's famous poem 'The Rime of the Ancient Mariner' (1798) is an example of the use of the Wandering Jew in the Romantic period.

2. *The History of Nourjahad* (1767) by Frances Sheridan (1724–66) describes how Nourjahad is tricked by the sultan Schemzeddin into believing that he has become immortal and that his periods of sleep last for several years at a time.

3. Cornelius Agrippa (1486–1535) was a German cabalist, and author of *De Occulta Philosophia Libri Tres* (1529).

4. Robert Southey (1774–1843) narrates the supposedly true story of Cornelius Agrippa's disobedient apprentice in his poem 'Cornelius Agrippa' (1799).

5. See the Gospel According to St Luke (4:24).

6. 'Nestors', meaning the elderly contingent of a village, is a reference to the Homeric hero Nestor, famous for his age and wisdom.

The Evil Eye

The wild Albanian kirtled to his knee,
With shawl-girt head, and ornamented gun,
And gold-embroidered garments, fair to see;
The crimson-scarfed man of Macedon.

Lord Byron[1]

The Moreot[2], Katusthius Ziani, travelled wearily, and in fear of its robber inhabitants, through the pashalik[3] of Ioannina[4]; yet he had no cause for dread. Did he arrive, tired and hungry, in a solitary village – did he find himself in the uninhabited wilds suddenly surrounded by a band of klephts[5] – or in the larger towns did he shrink at finding himself sole of his race among the savage mountaineers and despotic Turks? As soon as he announced himself the *pobratimo*[a] of Dmitri of the Evil Eye, every hand was held out, every voice spoke welcome.

The Albanian, Dmitri, was a native of the village of Corvo. Among the savage mountains of the district between Ioannina and Tepelene, the deep broad stream of Argyrocastro flows; bastioned to the west by abrupt wood-covered precipices, shadowed to the east by elevated mountains. The highest among these is Mount Trebucci; and in a romantic folding of that hill, distinct with minarets, crowned by a dome rising from out a group of pyramidal cypresses, is the picturesque village of Corvo. Sheep and goats form the apparent treasure of its inhabitants; their guns and yataghans[6], their warlike habits and, with them,

a. In Greece, especially in Illyria and Epirus, it is no uncommon thing for persons of the same sex to swear friendship. The Church contains a ritual to consecrate this vow. Two men thus united are called *pobratimi*; the women *posestrime*.

the noble profession of robbery, are sources of still greater wealth. Among a race renowned for dauntless courage and sanguinary enterprise, Dmitri was distinguished.

It was said that in his youth this klepht was remarkable for a gentler disposition and more refined taste than is usual with his countrymen. He had been a wanderer, and had learnt European arts, of which he was not a little proud. He could read and write Greek, and a book was often stowed beside his pistols in his girdle. He had spent several years in Scio[7], the most civilised of the Greek islands, and had married a Sciote girl. The Albanians are characterised as despisers of women; but Dmitri, in becoming the husband of Helena, enlisted under a more chivalrous rule, and became the proselyte of a better creed. Often he returned to his native hills, and fought under the banner of the renowned Ali[8], and then came back to his island home. The love of the tamed barbarian was concentrated, burning, and something beyond this – it was a portion of his living, beating heart – the nobler part of himself – the diviner mould in which his rugged nature had been recast.

On his return from one of his Albanian expeditions, he found his home ravaged by the Mainotes[9]. Helena – they pointed to her tomb, nor dared tell him how she died; his only child, his lovely infant daughter, was stolen; his treasure house of love and happiness was rifled; its gold-excelling wealth changed to blank desolation. Dmitri spent three years in endeavours to recover his lost offspring. He was exposed to a thousand dangers; underwent incredible hardships. He dared the wild beast in his lair, the Mainote in his port of refuge; he attacked, and was attacked by them. He wore the badge of his daring in a deep gash across his eyebrow and cheek. On this occasion he had died, but that Katusthius, seeing a scuffle on shore and a man left for dead, disembarked from a Moreot sacoleva [10], carried him away, tended and cured him. They exchanged vows of friendship, and for some time the Albanian shared his brother's toils; but they were too pacific to suit his taste, and he returned to Corvo.

Who in the mutilated savage could recognise the handsomest amongst the Arnaoots[11]? His habits kept pace with his change of physiognomy – he grew ferocious and hard-hearted – he only smiled when engaged in dangerous enterprise; he had arrived at that worst state of ruffian feeling, the taking delight in blood. He grew old in these occupations; his mind became reckless, his countenance more dark; men trembled before his glance, women and children exclaimed in terror, 'The Evil Eye!' The opinion became prevalent – he shared it himself – he gloried in the dread privilege; and when his victim shivered and withered beneath the mortal influence, the fiendish laugh with which he hailed this demonstration of his power struck with worse dismay the failing heart of the fascinated person. But Dmitri could command the arrows of his sight; and his comrades respected him the more for his supernatural attribute, since they did not fear the exercise of it on themselves.

Dmitri had just returned from an expedition beyond Preveza. He and his comrades were laden with spoil. They killed and roasted a goat whole for their repast; they drank dry several wineskins; then, round the fire in the court, they abandoned themselves to the delights of the kerchief dance, roaring out the chorus as they dropped upon and then rebounded from their knees, and whirled round and round with an activity all their own. The heart of Dmitri was heavy; he refused to dance, and sat apart, at first joining in the song with his voice and lute, till the air changed to one that reminded him of better days; his voice died away – his instrument dropped from his hands – and his head sank upon his breast.

At the sound of stranger footsteps he started up; in the form before him he surely recognised a friend – he was not mistaken. With a joyful exclamation he welcomed Katusthius Ziani, clasping his hand, and kissing him on his cheek. The traveller was weary, so they retired to Dmitri's own home – a neatly plastered, whitewashed cottage whose earthen floor was perfectly dry and clean, and the walls hung with arms, some richly ornamented, and other trophies of his klephtic triumphs. A fire was kindled by his aged female attendant; the friends reposed on mats of white rushes, while she prepared the pilaf and seethed flesh of kid. She placed a bright tin tray on a block of wood before them, and heaped upon it cakes of Indian corn, goat's-milk cheese, eggs and olives; a jar of water from their purest spring, and skin of wine, served to refresh and cheer the thirsty traveller.

After supper, the guest spoke of the object of his visit. 'I come to my *pobratimo*,' he said, 'to claim the performance of his vow. When I rescued you from the savage Kakov-ougnis of Boularias, you pledged to me your gratitude and faith; do you disclaim the debt?'

Dmitri's brow darkened. 'My brother,' he cried, 'need not remind me of what I owe. Command my life –

in what can the mountain klepht aid the son of the worthy Ziani?'

'The son of Ziani is a beggar,' rejoined Katusthius, 'and must perish if his brother deny his assistance.'

The Moreot then told his tale. He had been brought up as the only son of a rich merchant of Corinth. He had often sailed as caravokeiri[a] of his father's vessels to Istanbul, and even to Calabria. Some years before, he had been boarded and taken by a Barbary corsair.[12] His life since then had been adventurous, he said; in truth, it had been a guilty one – he had become a renegade – and won regard from his new allies, not by his superior courage, for he was cowardly, but by the frauds that make men worthy. In the midst of this career some superstition had influenced him, and he had returned to his ancient religion. He escaped from Africa, wandered through Syria, crossed to Europe, found occupation in Constantinople; and thus years passed. At last, as he was on the point of marriage with a Fanariote[13] beauty, he fell again into poverty, and he returned to Corinth to see if his father's fortunes had prospered during his long wanderings. He found that while these had improved to a wonder, they were lost to him for ever. His father, during his protracted absence, acknowledged another son as his; and, dying a year before, had left all to him. Katusthius found this unknown kinsman, with his wife and child, in possession of his expected inheritance. Cyril divided with him, it is true, their parent's property; but Katusthius grasped at all, and resolved to obtain it. He brooded over a thousand schemes of murder and

a. The master of a merchant ship.

revenge; yet the blood of a brother was sacred to him; and Cyril, beloved and respected at Corinth, could only be attacked with considerable risk. Then his child was a fresh obstacle. As the best plan that presented itself, he hastily embarked for Butrint[14], and came to claim the advice and assistance of the Arnaoot whose life he had saved, whose *pobratimo* he was. Not thus barely did he tell his tale, but glossed it over; so that had Dmitri needed the incitement of justice, which was not at all a desideratum with him, he would have been satisfied that Cyril was a base interloper, and that the whole transaction was one of imposture and villainy.

All night these men discussed a variety of projects whose aim was that the deceased Ziani's wealth should pass undivided into his elder son's hands. At morning's dawn Katusthius departed, and two days afterwards Dmitri quitted his mountain home. His first care had been to purchase a horse, long coveted by him on account of its beauty and fleetness; he provided cartridges, and replenished his powder-horn. His accoutrements were rich, his dress gay; his arms glittered in the sun. His long hair fell straight from under the shawl twisted round his cap, even to his waist; a shaggy white capote hung from his shoulder; his face wrinkled and puckered by exposure to the seasons; his brow furrowed with care; his mustachios long and jet-black; his scarred face; his wild, savage eyes; his whole appearance, not deficient in barbaric grace, but stamped chiefly with ferocity and bandit pride, inspired – and we need not wonder – the superstitious Greek with a belief that a supernatural spirit of evil dwelt in his aspect, blasting and destroying. Now the land, chimed in with the last song of the noisy cicada; the rippling waves spent themselves almost silently among the shingles. This was his home; but where its lovely flower? Zella did not come forth to welcome him. A domestic pointed to a chapel on a neighbouring acclivity, and there he found her; his child (nearly three years of age) was in his nurse's arms; his wife was praying fervently, while the tears streamed down her cheeks. Cyril demanded anxiously the meaning of this scene; but the nurse sobbed; Zella continued to pray and weep; and the boy, from sympathy, began to cry. This was too much for man to endure. Cyril left the chapel; he leant against a walnut tree. His first exclamation was a customary Greek one – 'Welcome this misfortune, so that it come single!' But what was the ill that had occurred? Unapparent was it yet; but the spirit of evil is most fatal when unseen. He was happy – a lovely wife, a blooming child, a peaceful home, competence, and the prospect of wealth; these blessings were his: yet how often does Fortune use such as her decoys? He was a slave in an enslaved land, a mortal subject to the high destinies, and ten thousand were the envenomed darts which might be hurled at his devoted head. Now timid and trembling, Zella came from the chapel: her explanation did not calm his fears. Again the Evil Eye had been on his child, and deep malignity lurked surely under this second visitation. The same man, an Arnaoot, with glittering arms, gay attire, mounted on a black steed, came from the neighbouring ilex grove, and, riding furiously up to the door, suddenly checked and reined in his horse at the very threshold. The child ran towards him: the Arnaoot bent his sinister eyes upon him:

Zella was unwilling to quit her home, even for a short interval; but she suffered herself to be persuaded, and they proceeded altogether for several miles towards the capital of the Morea. At noontide they made a repast under the shadow of a grove of oaks, and then separated. Returning homeward, the wedded pair congratulated themselves on their tranquil life and peaceful happiness, contrasted with the wanderer's lonely and homeless pleasures. These feelings increased in intensity as they drew nearer their dwelling, and anticipated the lisped welcome of their idolised child. From an eminence they looked upon the fertile vale which was their home – it was situated on the southern side of the isthmus, and looked upon the Gulf of Aegina – all was verdant, tranquil, and beautiful. They descended into the plain; there a singular appearance attracted their attention. A plough with its yoke of oxen had been deserted midway in the furrow; the animals had dragged it to the side of the field, and endeavoured to repose as well as their conjunction permitted. The sun already touched its western bourne, and the summits of the trees were gilded by its parting beams. All was silent; even the eternal waterwheel was still; no menials appeared at their usual rustic labours. From the house the voice of wailing was too plainly heard. 'My child!' Zella exclaimed. Cyril began to reassure her; but another lament arose, and he hurried on. She dismounted, and would have followed him, but sank on the roadside. Her husband returned. 'Courage, my beloved,' he cried; 'I will not repose night or day until Constans is restored to us – trust to me – farewell!' With these words he rode swiftly on.

Her worst fears were thus confirmed; her maternal

heart, lately so joyous, became the abode of despair, while the nurse's narration of the sad occurrence tended but to add worse fear to fear.

Thus it was: the same stranger of the Evil Eye had appeared, not as before, bearing down on them with eagle speed, but as if from a long journey; his horse lame and with drooping head; the Arnaoot himself covered with dust, apparently scarcely able to keep his seat. 'By the life of your child,' he said, 'give a cup of water to one who faints with thirst.' The nurse, with Constans in her arms, got a bowl of the desired liquid, and presented it. Before the parched lips of the stranger touched the wave, the vessel fell from his hands. The women started back, while he, at the same moment darting forwards, tore with strong arm the child from her embrace. Already both were gone – with arrowy speed they traversed the plain, while her shrieks and cries for assistance called together all the domestics. They followed on the track of the ravisher, and none had yet returned. Now, as night closed in, one by one they came back; they had nothing to relate; they had scoured the woods, crossed the hills – they could not even discover the route which the Albanian had taken.

On the following day Cyril returned, jaded, haggard, miserable; he had obtained no tidings of his son. On the morrow he again departed on his quest, nor came back for several days. Zella passed her time wearily – now sitting in hopeless despondency, now climbing the near hill to see whether she could perceive the approach of her husband. She was not allowed to remain long thus tranquil; the trembling domestics, left in guard, warned her that the savage forms of several Arnaoots had been seen prowling about. She herself saw a tall figure, clad in a shaggy white capote, steal round the promontory and, on seeing her, shrink back. Once at night the snorting and trampling of a horse roused her, not from slumber, but from her sense of security. Wretched as the bereft mother was, she felt personally almost reckless of danger; but she was not her own, she belonged to one beyond expression dear; and duty, as well as affection for him, enjoined self-preservation. He, Cyril, again returned: he was gloomier, sadder than before; but there was more resolution on his brow, more energy in his motions; he had obtained a clue, yet it might only lead him to the depths of despair.

He discovered that Katusthius had not embarked at Naples. He had joined a band of Arnaoots lurking about Vasilico, and had proceeded to Patras[18] with the protoklepht; thence they put off together in a mon-oxylon[19] for the northern shores of the Gulf of Lepanto[20]: nor were they alone; they bore a child with them wrapped in a heavy torpid sleep. Poor Cyril's blood ran cold when he thought of the spells and witchcraft which had probably been put in practice on his boy. He would have followed close upon the robbers, but for the report that reached him that the remainder of the Albanians had proceeded southward towards Corinth. He could not enter upon a long wandering search among the pathless wilds of Epirus[21], leaving Zella exposed to the attacks of these bandits. He returned to consult with her, to devise some plan of action which at once ensured her safety, and promised success to his endeavours.

After some hesitation and discussion, it was decided that he should first conduct her to her native home, consult with her father as to his present enterprise, and be guided by his warlike experience before he rushed into the very focus of danger. The seizure of his child might only be a lure, and it were not well for him, sole protector of that child and its mother, to rush unadvisedly into the toils.

Zella, strange to say, for her blue eyes and brilliant complexion belied her birth, was the daughter of a Mainote: yet dreaded and abhorred by the rest of the world as are the inhabitants of Cape Taenarus, they are celebrated for their domestic virtues and the strength of their private attachments. Zella loved her father and the memory of her rugged rocky home, from which she had been torn in an adverse hour. Near neighbours of the Mainotes, dwelling in the ruder and most incult portion of Maina, are the Kakovougnis, a dark suspicious race, of squat and stunted form, strongly contrasted with the tranquil cast of countenance characteristic of the Mainote. The two tribes are embroiled in perpetual quarrels; the narrow sea-girt abode which they share affords at once a secure place of refuge from the foreign enemy, and all the facilities of internal mountain warfare. Cyril had once, during a coasting voyage, been driven by stress of weather into the little bay on whose shores is placed the small town of Kardamyla. The crew at first dreaded to be captured by the pirates; but they were reassured on finding them fully occupied by their domestic dissensions. A band of Kakovougnis were besieging the castellated rock overlooking Kardamyla, blockading the fortress in which the Mainote captain and his family had taken refuge. Two days passed thus, while furious contrary winds detained Cyril in the bay.

On the third evening the western gale subsided, and a land breeze promised to emancipate them from their perilous condition; when in the night, as they were about to put off in a boat from shore, they were hailed by a party of Mainotes, and one, an old man of commanding figure, demanded a parley. He was the captain of Kardamyla, the chief of the fortress now attacked by his implacable enemies: he saw no escape – he must fall – and his chief desire was to save his treasure and his family from the hands of his enemies. Cyril consented to receive them on board: the latter consisted of an old mother, a paramana, and a young and beautiful girl, his daughter. Cyril conducted them in safety to Naples. Soon after, the captain's mother and paramana returned to their native town, while, with her father's consent, fair Zella became the wife of her preserver. The fortunes of the Mainote had prospered since then, and he stood first in rank, the chief of a large tribe, the captain of Kardamyla.

Thither then the hapless parents repaired; they embarked on board a small sacoleva, which dropped down the Gulf of Aegina, weathered the islands of Skvllo and Cerigo, and the extreme point of Taerus: favoured by prosperous gales, they made the desired port, and arrived at the hospitable mansion of old Camaraz. He heard their tale with indignation; swore by his beard to dip his poniard in the best blood of Katusthius, and insisted upon accompanying his son-in-law on his expedition to Albania. No time was lost – the grey-headed mariner, still full of energy, hastened every preparation. Cyril and Zella parted; a thousand fears, a thousand hours of misery rose between the pair, late sharers in perfect happiness. The boisterous sea and distant lands were the smallest of the obstacles that divided them; they would not fear the worst; yet hope, a sickly plant, faded in their hearts as they tore themselves asunder after a last embrace.

Zella returned from the fertile district of Corinth to her barren native rocks. She felt all joy expire as she viewed from the rugged shore the lessening sails of the sacoleva. Days and weeks passed, and still she remained in solitary and sad expectation: she never joined in the dance, nor made one in the assemblies of her countrywomen, who met together at evening-tide to sing, tell stories, and while away the time in dance and gaiety. She secluded herself in the most lonely part of her father's house, and gazed unceasingly from the lattice upon the sea beneath, or wandered on the rocky beach; and when tempest darkened the sky, and each precipitous promontory grew purple under the shadows of the wide-winged clouds, when the roar of the surges was on the shore, and the white crests of the waves, seen afar upon the ocean plain, showed like flocks of newly shorn sheep scattered along wide-extended downs, she felt neither gale nor inclement cold, nor returned home till recalled by her attendants. In obedience to them she sought the shelter of her abode, not to remain long; for the wild winds spoke to her, and the stormy ocean reproached her tranquillity. Unable to control the impulse, she would rush from her habitation on the cliff, nor remember, till she reached the shore, that her papooshes[22] were left midway on the mountain path, and that her forgotten veil and disordered dress were unmeet for such a scene. Often the unnumbered hours sped on, while this orphaned child of happiness leant on a cold dark rock; the low-browed crags beetled over her, the surges broke at her feet, her fair limbs were stained by spray, her tresses dishevelled by the gale. Hopelessly she wept until a sail appeared on the horizon; and then she dried her fast flowing tears, fixing her large eyes upon the nearing hull or fading topsail. Meanwhile the storm tossed the clouds into a thousand gigantic shapes, and the tumultuous sea grew blacker and more wild; her natural gloom was heightened by superstitious horror. The Moirae, the old fates of her native Grecian soil, howled in the breezes; apparitions, which told of her child pining under the influence of the Evil Eye, and of her husband – the prey of some Thracian[23] witchcraft, such as still is practised in the dread neighbourhood of Larisa – haunted her broken slumbers, and stalked like dire shadows across her waking thoughts. Her bloom was gone, her eyes lost their lustre, her limbs their round full beauty; her strength failed her as she tottered to the accustomed spot to watch – vainly, yet forever to watch.

What is there so fearful as the expectation of evil tidings delayed? Sometimes in the midst of tears, or worse, amidst the convulsive gaspings of despair, we reproach ourselves for influencing the eternal fates by our gloomy anticipations: then, if a smile wreathe the mourner's quivering lip, it is arrested by a throb of agony. Alas! Are not the dark tresses of the young painted grey; the full cheek of beauty delved with sad lines by the spirits of such hours? Misery is a more welcome visitant when she comes in her darkest guise and wraps us in perpetual black, for then the heart no longer sickens with disappointed hope.

Cyril and old Camaraz had found great difficulty in

Acroceraunia, to the east, west, north, and south, close in the various prospects. Cyril half envied the Caloyers their inert tranquillity. They received the travellers gladly, and were cordial though simple in their manners. When questioned concerning the object of their journey, they warmly sympathised with the father's anxiety, and eagerly told all they knew. Two weeks before, an Arnaoot, well known to them as Dmitri of the Evil Eye, a famous klepht of Corvo, and a Moreot, arrived, bringing with them a child – a bold, spirited, beautiful boy who, with firmness beyond his years, claimed the protection of the Caloyers, and accused his companions of having carried him off by force from his parents. 'By my head!' cried the Albanian, 'a brave Palikar[25]: he keeps his word, brother; he swore by the Panagia[26], in spite of our threats of throwing him down a precipice, food for the vulture, to accuse us to the first good men he saw: he neither pines under the Evil Eye, nor quails beneath our menaces.' Katusthius frowned at these praises, and it became evident during their stay at the monastery that the Albanian and the Moreot quarrelled as to the disposal of the child. The rugged mountaineer threw off all his sternness as he gazed upon the boy. When little Constans slept, he hung over him, fanning away, with woman's care, the flies and gnats. When he spoke, he answered with expressions of fondness, winning him with gifts, teaching him, all baby as he was, a mimicry of warlike exercises. When the boy knelt and besought the Panagia to restore him to his parents, his infant voice quivering, and tears running down his cheeks, the eyes of Dmitri overflowed; he cast his cloak over his face; his heart whispered to him: 'Thus, perhaps, my child prayed. Heaven was deaf – alas! Where is she now?' Encouraged by such signs of compassion, which children are quick to perceive, Constans twined his arms round his neck, telling him that he loved him, and that he would fight for him when a man, if he would take him back to Corinth. At such words Dmitri would rush forth, seek Katusthius, remonstrate with him, till the unrelenting man checked him by reminding him of his vow. Still he swore that no hair of the child's head should be injured; while the uncle, unvisited by compunction, meditated his destruction. The quarrels which thence arose were frequent and violent, till Katusthius, weary of opposition, had recourse to craft to obtain his purpose. One night he secretly left the monastery, bearing the child with him. When Dmitri heard of his evasion, it was a fearful thing to the good Caloyers only to look upon him; they instinctively clutched hold of every bit of iron on which they could lay their hands so to avert the Evil Eye which glared with native and untamed fierceness. In their panic a whole score of them had rushed to the iron-plated door which led out of their abode: with the strength of a lion, Dmitri tore them away, threw back the portal, and with the swiftness of a torrent fed by the thawing of the snows in spring, he dashed down the steep hill: the flight of an eagle not more rapid; the course of a wild beast not more resolved.

Such was the clue afforded to Cyril. It were too long to follow him in his subsequent search; he, with old Camaraz, wandered through the vale of Argyrocastro, and climbed Mount Trebucci to Corvo. Dmitri had returned; he had gathered together a score of faithful comrades, and sallied forth again; various were the reports of his destination and the enterprise which he meditated.

One of these led our adventurers to Tepelene, and hence back towards Ioannina, and now chance again favoured them. They rested one night in the habitation of a priest at the little village of Mosme, about three leagues to the north of Zitsa; and here they found an Arnaoot who had been disabled by a fall from his horse; this man was to have made one of Dmitri's band: they learnt from him that the Arnaoot had tracked Katusthius, following him close, and forcing him to take refuge in the monastery of the Prophet Elias, which stands on an elevated peak of the mountains of Sagori, eight leagues from Ioannina. Dmitri had followed him, and demanded the child. The Caloyers refused to give it up, and the klepht, roused to mad indignation, was now besieging and battering the monastery to obtain by force this object of his newly awakened affections.

At Ioannina, Camaraz and Cyril collected their comrades, and departed to join their unconscious ally. He, more impetuous than a mountain stream or ocean's fiercest waves, struck terror into the hearts of the recluses by his ceaseless and dauntless attacks. To encourage them to further resistance, Katusthius, leaving the child behind in the monastery, departed for the nearest town of Sagori to entreat its Belouk-Bashee to come to their aid. The Sagorians are a mild, amiable, social people; they are gay, frank, clever; their bravery is universally acknowledged, even by the more uncivilised mountaineers of Zoumerkas; yet robbery, murder, and other acts of violence, are unknown among them. These good people were not a little indignant when they heard that a band of Arnaoots was besieging and battering the sacred retreat of their favourite Caloyers. They assembled in a gallant troop, and taking Katusthius with them, hastened to drive the insolent klephts back to their ruder fastnesses. They came too late. At midnight, while the monks prayed fervently to be delivered from their enemies, Dmitri and his followers tore down their iron-plated door, and entered the holy precincts. The protoklepht strode up to the gates of the sanctuary, and placing his hands upon it, swore that he came to save, not to destroy. Constans saw him. With a cry of delight he disengaged himself from the Caloyer who held him, and rushed into his arms: this was sufficient triumph. With assurances of sincere regret for having disturbed them, the klepht quitted the chapel with his followers, taking his prize with him.

Katusthius returned some hours after, and so well did the traitor plead his cause with the kind Sagorians, bewailing the fate of his little nephew among these evil men, that they offered to follow, and, superior as their numbers were, to rescue the boy from their destructive hands. Katusthius, delighted with the proposition, urged their immediate departure. At dawn they began to climb the mountain summits, already trodden by the Zoumerkians.

Delighted with repossessing his little favourite, Dmitri placed him before him on his horse, and, followed by his comrades, made his way over the elevated mountains, clothed with old Dodona's[27] oaks, or, in higher summits, by dark gigantic pines. They proceeded for some hours, and at length dismounted to repose. The spot they chose was the depth of a dark ravine, whose gloom was increased by the broad shadows of dark ilexes; an entangled underwood, and a sprinkling of craggy isolated rocks, made it difficult for the horses to keep their footing. They dismounted, and sat by the little stream. Their simple fare was spread, and Dmitri enticed the boy to eat by a thousand caresses. Suddenly one of his men, set as a guard, brought intelligence that a troop of Sagorians, with Katusthius as their guide, was advancing from the monastery of St Elias; while another man gave the alarm of the approach of six or eight well-armed Moreots who were advancing on the road from Ioannina; in a moment every sign of encampment had disappeared. The Arnaoots began to climb the hills, getting under cover of the rocks, and behind the large trunks of the forest trees, keeping concealed till their invaders should be in the very midst of them. Soon the Moreots appeared, turning round the defile, in a path that only allowed them to proceed two by two; they were unaware of danger, and walked carelessly, until a shot that whizzed over the head of one, striking the bough of a tree, recalled them from their security.

The Greeks, accustomed to the same mode of warfare, betook themselves also to the safeguards of the rocks, firing from behind them, striving with their adversaries which should get to the most elevated station; jumping from crag to crag, and dropping down and firing as quickly as they could load: one old man alone remained on the pathway. The mariner, Camaraz, had often encountered the enemy on the deck of his kayak, and would still have rushed foremost at a boarding, but this warfare

74

required too much activity. Cyril called on him to shelter himself beneath a low, broad stone: the Mainote waved his hand. 'Fear not for me,' he cried; 'I know how to die!' The brave love the brave. Dmitri saw the old man stand, unflinching, a mark for all the balls, and he started from behind his rocky screen, calling on his men to cease. Then addressing his enemy, he cried, 'Who are you? Why are you here? If you come in peace, proceed on your way. Answer, and fear not!'

The old man drew himself up, saying, 'I am a Mainote, and cannot fear. All Hellas trembles before the pirates of Cape Matapan[28], and I am one of these! I do not come in peace! Behold! You have in your arms the cause of our dissension! I am the grandsire of that child – give him to me!'

Dmitri, had he held a snake, which he felt awakening in his bosom, could not so suddenly have changed his cheer: 'the offspring of a Mainote!', he relaxed his grasp; Constans would have fallen had he not clung to his neck. Meanwhile each party had descended from their rocky station, and were grouped together in the pathway below. Dmitri tore the child from his neck; he felt as if he could, with savage delight, dash him down the precipice – when, as he paused and trembled from excess of passion, Katusthius, and the foremost Sagorians, came down upon them.

'Stand!' cried the infuriated Arnaoot. 'Behold Katusthius! Behold, friend, whom I, driven by the resistless fates, madly and wickedly forswore! I now perform your wish – the Mainote child dies! The son of the accursed race shall be the victim of my just revenge!'

Cyril, in a transport of fear, rushed up the rock; he levelled his musket, but he feared to sacrifice his child. The old Mainote, less timid and more desperate, took a steady aim; Dmitri saw the act, and hurled the dagger, already raised against the child, at him – it entered his side – while Constans, feeling his late protector's grasp relax, sprung from it into his father's arms.

Camaraz had fallen, yet his wound was slight. He saw the Arnaoots and Sagorians close round him; he saw his own followers made prisoners. Dmitri and Katusthius had both thrown themselves upon Cyril, struggling to repossess themselves of the screaming boy. The Mainote raised himself – he was feeble of limb, but his heart was strong; he threw himself before the father and child; he caught the upraised arm of Dmitri. 'On me,' he cried, 'falls all your vengeance! I of the evil race! For the child, he is innocent of such parentage! Maina cannot boast him for a son!'

'Man of lies!' commenced the infuriated Arnaoot, 'this falsehood shall not stead thee!'

'Nay, by the souls of those you have loved, listen!' continued Camaraz. 'And if I make not good my words, may I and my children die! The boy's father is a Corinthian – his mother, a Sciote girl!'

'Scio!' the very word made the blood recede to Dmitri's heart. 'Villain!' he cried, dashing aside Katusthius' arm, which was raised against poor Constans, 'I guard this child – dare not to injure him! Speak, old man, and fear not, so that you speakest the truth.'

'Fifteen years ago,' said Camaraz, 'I hovered with my kayak, in search of prey, on the coast of Scio. A cottage stood on the borders of a chestnut wood, it was the habitation of the widow of a worthy islander – she dwelt in it with her only daughter, married to an Albanian, then absent; the good woman was reported to have a concealed treasure in her house – the girl herself would be rich spoil – it was an adventure worth the risk. We ran our vessel up a shady creek, and, on the going down of the moon, landed; stealing under the covert of night towards the lonely abode of these women.'

Dmitri grasped at his dagger's hilt – it was no longer there; he half drew a pistol from his girdle; little Constans, again confiding in his former friend, stretched out his infant hands and clung to his arm; the klepht looked on him, half yielded to his desire to embrace him, half feared to be deceived; so he turned away, throwing his capote over his face, veiling his anguish, controlling his emotions, till all should be told. Camaraz continued:

'It became a worse tragedy than I had contemplated. The girl had a child – she feared for its life, and struggled with the men like a tigress defending her young. I was in another room seeking for the hidden store, when a piercing shriek rent the air – I never knew what compassion was before – this cry went to my heart – but it was too late, the poor girl had sunk to the ground, the life-tide oozing from her bosom. I know not why, but I turned woman in my regret for the slain beauty. I meant to have carried her and her child on board, to see if anything could be done to save her, but she died before we left the shore. I thought she would like her island grave best, and truly feared that she might turn vampire to haunt me did I carry her away; so we left her corpse for the priests to bury, and carried off the child, then about two years old. She could say few words except her own name, that was Zella, and she is the mother of this boy!'

* * * *

A succession of arrivals in the bay of Kardamyla had kept poor Zella watching for many nights. Her attendant had, in despair of ever seeing her sleep again, drugged with opium the few cakes she persuaded her to eat, but the poor woman did not calculate on the power of mind over body, of love over every enemy, physical or moral, arrayed against it. Zella lay on her couch, her spirit somewhat subdued, but her heart alive, her eyes unclosed. In the night, led by some unexplained impulse, she crawled to her lattice, and saw a little sacoleva enter the bay; it ran in swiftly, under favour of the wind, and was lost to her sight under a jutting crag. Lightly she trod the marble floor of her chamber; she drew a large shawl close round her; she descended the rocky pathway, and reached, with swift steps, the beach – still the vessel was invisible, and she was half inclined to think that it was the offspring of her excited imagination – yet she lingered.

She felt a sickness at her very heart whenever she attempted to move, and her eyelids weighed down in spite of herself. The desire of sleep at last became irresistible; she lay down on the shingles, reposed her head on the cold, hard pillow, folded her shawl still closer, and gave herself up to forgetfulness.

So profoundly did she slumber under the influence of the opiate that for many hours she was insensible of any change in her situation. By degrees only she awoke, by degrees only became aware of the objects around her; the breeze felt fresh and free – so was it ever on the wave-beaten coast; the waters rippled near, their dash had been in her ears as she yielded to repose; but this was not her stony couch, that canopy, not the dark overhanging cliff. Suddenly she lifted up her head – she was on the deck of a small vessel, which was skimming swiftly over the ocean waves – a cloak of sables pillowed her head; the shores of Cape Matapan were to her left, and they steered right towards the noonday sun. Wonder rather than fear possessed her: with a quick hand she drew aside the sail that veiled her from the crew – the dreaded Albanian was sitting close at her side, her Constans cradled in his arms – she uttered a cry – Cyril turned at the sound, and in a moment she was folded in his embrace.

NOTES

1. From *Childe Harold's Pilgrimage* (1812–1818) by Byron (1788–1824), II. I. viii. The first two cantos of this four-canto poem describe the pilgrim's travels through Portugal, Spain, the Ionian Islands, and Albania. When writing 'The Evil Eye' – so unlike her other stories in terms of themes and setting – Mary Shelley was influenced by several contemporary examples of Eastern narratives. These included the second canto of *Childe Harold* (1812), Thomas Hope's *Anastasius* (1819) and Prosper Mérimée's *La Guzla* (1827) – a collection of folk ballads purporting to be translated from the original Illyrian, but later revealed by Mérimée to be a hoax. It this work in particular that seems to have inspired the Greek/Albanian setting of 'The Evil Eye'. Mary reviewed *La Guzla* for *The Westminster Review* in January 1829, ten months before her own story first appeared in *The Keepsake*.

2. A native inhabitant of the Peloponnese peninsula in Greece.

3. A district governed by a 'pasha' – a Turkish officer or governor of a province.

4. Ioannina (also Yannina or Janina) is a city in north-western Greece, and the administrative centre of the Epirus region.

5. Greek brigands or bandits.

6. A type of sword, often with a double-curved blade.

7. The Italian spelling for the Greek island, Chios.

8. Ali Pasha (1741–1822), known as the Lion of Ioannina.

9. Maina was the gathering place for Greek troops who fought for independence under their leader, Ypsilanti. In his poem *The Giaour* (1813) Byron likens the Mainotes to 'island-pirates'.

10. A small fishing boat.

11. The Arnaoots (or Arnauts) were a band of Albanian mountaineers. Byron refers to them in his poem *The Giaour* (see note 9).

12. Barbary corsairs were pirates from the Barbary coast of North Africa.

13. Fanar (or Phanar) was the Greek quarter of Constantinople (now Istanbul). Under the Ottoman Empire, Phanar was the residence of the privileged Greek families called Fanairotes (or Phanariots). They came to prominence in the late seventeenth century and held influential positions until the Greek War of Independence began in 1821.

14. The city of Butrint (now an archaeological site) is in the far south of Albania, just ten kilometres from the Greek island of Corfu.

15. An area in western Greece, to the west of Aetolia.

16. The medieval name for the Peloponnese peninsula, which is linked with central Greece by the Isthmus of Corinth.

17. See note 13.

18. Patras is the largest city in the Peloponnese.

19. A small boat or canoe made from one piece of wood.

20. The Gulf of Lepanto is a long arm of the Ionian sea, running from east to west and separating the Peloponnese peninsula to the south from the Greek mainland to the north.

21. Epirus is a mountainous area in the north-west corner of Greece.

22. Turkish slippers.

23. Of or concerned with Thrace – an ancient country lying to the west of the Black Sea and north of the Aegean.

24. From *Childe Harold's Pilgrimage* (see note 1), II. xlviii.

25. A member of the band of a Greek or Albanian military chief during the War of Independence.

26. The Church of Panagia of Blachernae was the best-known and most celebrated shrine of the Holy Virgin in Constantinople.

27. The ancient site of Dodona is located twenty-two kilometres south of Ioannina.

28. Cape Matapan lies off the Peloponnese coast.

Mary Shelley was born in London in 1797, the only daughter of the radical writers William Godwin and Mary Wollstonecraft. Her mother died just a few days after her birth. In 1814, at the age of seventeen, Mary left England with the writer Percy Bysshe Shelley, whom she eventually married in 1816 after the suicide of his first wife, Harriet. She spent the summer of 1816 at Lake Geneva with Shelley, Lord Byron, and John Polidori and it was here that Mary began *Frankenstein, or the Modern Prometheus*, the novel for which she is best remembered. *Frankenstein* was published in 1818 and followed by *Valperga* in 1823 and the futuristic novel, *The Last Man*, in 1826. She wrote other novels, including *Lodore*, published in 1835, as well as several biographies and numerous short stories; many with supernatural and science-fiction themes. Her novella, *Matilda*, with its controversial subject of an incestuous father/daughter relationship remained unpublished until 1959.

After Shelley was drowned in August 1823, Mary Shelley left Italy and moved back to England, where she was to remain for the rest of her life. Although widowed at the young age of twenty-five, she did not remarry. Only the youngest of her three children, Percy, survived infancy, Clara and William ('Willmouse') having died in Italy in 1818 and 1819 respectively. In later life, Mary edited her husband's poems, essays and letters. Renouncing many of the radical views she held in earlier life, she died in February 1851.

HESPERUS PRESS CLASSICS

Hesperus Press, as suggested by the Latin motto, is committed to bringing near what is far – far both in space and time. Works written by the greatest authors, and unjustly neglected or simply little known in the English-speaking world, are made accessible through new translations and a completely fresh editorial approach. Through these classic works, the reader is introduced to the greatest writers from all times and all cultures.

For more information on Hesperus Press, please visit our website: **www.hesperuspress.com**

ET REMOTISSIMA PROPE

SELECTED TITLES FROM HESPERUS PRESS

Author	Title	Foreword writer
Louisa May Alcott	*Behind a Mask*	Doris Lessing
Pedro Antonio de Alarcon	*The Three-Cornered Hat*	
Pietro Aretino	*The School of Whoredom*	Paul Bailey
Pietro Aretino	*The Secret Life of Nuns*	
Jane Austen	*Love and Friendship*	Fay Weldon
Honoré de Balzac	*Colonel Chabert*	A.N. Wilson
Charles Baudelaire	*On Wine and Hashish*	Margaret Drabble
Aphra Behn	*The Lover's Watch*	
Giovanni Boccaccio	*Life of Dante*	A.N. Wilson
Charlotte Brontë	*The Foundling*	
Charlotte Brontë	*The Green Dwarf*	Libby Purves
Emily Brontë	*Poems of Solitude*	Helen Dunmore
Mikhail Bulgakov	*The Fatal Eggs*	Doris Lessing
Giacomo Casanova	*The Duel*	Tim Parks
Miguel de Cervantes	*The Dialogue of the Dogs*	Ben Okri
Geoffrey Chaucer	*The Parliament of Birds*	
Anton Chekhov	*The Story of a Nobody*	Louis de Bernières
Anton Chekhov	*Three Years*	William Fiennes
Wilkie Collins	*The Frozen Deep*	
Wilkie Collins	*Who Killed Zebedee?*	Martin Jarvis
Arthur Conan Doyle	*The Mystery of Cloomber*	
Arthur Conan Doyle	*The Tragedy of the Korosko*	Tony Robinson
William Congreve	*Incognita*	Peter Ackroyd
Joseph Conrad	*Heart of Darkness*	A.N. Wilson
Joseph Conrad	*The Return*	Colm Tóibín
Gabriele D'Annunzio	*The Book of the Virgins*	Tim Parks
Xavier de Maistre	*Journey Around my Room*	Alain de Botton